WRITTEN BY JON SCIESZKA

CHARACTERS AND ENVIRONMENTS DEVELOPED BY THE

DAVID SHANNON   **LOREN LONG**   **DAVID GORDON**

ILLUSTRATION CREW:

Executive producer: TOT INDUSTRIES in association with Animagic S.L.

Creative supervisor: Sergio Pablos ◌ Drawings by: Juan Pablo Navas ◌ Color by: Isabel Nadal

Color assistant: Gabriela Lazbal ◌ Art director: Karin Paprocki

READY-TO-ROLL

ALADDIN PAPERBACKS
NEW YORK   LONDON   TORONTO   SYDNEY

ALADDIN PAPERBACKS

An imprint of Simon & Schuster Children's Publishing Division

1230 Avenue of the Americas, New York, NY 10020

Copyright © 2008 by Jon Scieszka

READY-TO-READ, ALADDIN PAPERBACKS, and related logo
are registered trademarks of Simon & Schuster, Inc.

TRUCKTOWN and JON SCIESZKA'S TRUCKTOWN and design are trademarks of JRS Worldwide, LLC.

The text of this book was set in Truck King.

Manufactured in the United States of America

First Aladdin Paperbacks edition June 2008

10 9 8 7 6 5 4 3 2 1

Library of Congress Cataloging-in-Publication Data

Scieszka, Jon.

Zoom! boom! bully / by Jon Scieszka ; artwork created by the Design Garage:

David Gordon, Loren Long, David Shannon.—1st Aladdin Paperbacks ed.

p. cm.—(Jon Scieszka's Trucktown. Ready-to-roll)

Summary: Big Rig loves to smash items delivered to a construction site,

including barrels, crates, tires, and even his own birthday presents.

ISBN-13: 978-1-4169-4139-2

ISBN-10: 1-4169-4139-8

[1. Trucks—Fiction. 2. Construction equipment—Fiction. 3. Bullies—Fiction.]

I. Design Garage. II. Gordon, David, 1965 Jan. 22- ill. III. Long, Loren, ill.

IV. Shannon, David, ill. V. Title.

PZ7.S41267Zo 2008   [E]—dc22   2007027258

Jack unloads **four** barrels.

"Big Rig!"

shouts Jack.

"He is **such** a bully," says Gabby.

Dan dumps out **three** crates.

"Big Rig!" says Melvin.
"I told you," says Gabby.
"He is such a bully."

Pete **SCOOPS**
two tires.

"Big Rig!" says Pete.

"I told you," says Gabby.

"We know," says Pete.
"He is such a bully."

Melvin decorates **One** cake.

"**STOP!**"
shouts Jack.
"This was all for you,
Big Rig."

"Happy birthday,"

say Dan and Pete
and Gabby and Melvin.

"Oh. **Really?**"
says Big Rig.
"Then **this** is my **best birthday ever!**"